weird and
wonderful

weird and wonderful

stories chosen by
wendy cooling

Dolphin

A Dolphin Paperback

First published in Great Britain in 1997
by Orion Children's Books
a division of the Orion Publishing Group Ltd
Orion House
5 Upper St Martin's Lane
London WC2H 9EA

A catalogue record for this book is available
from the British Library
Typeset by Deltatype Ltd, Birkenhead, Merseyside
Printed in Great Britain by Clays Ltd, St Ives plc
ISBN 1 85881 446 4

contents

the gingerbread house

adèle geras

I want to tell someone about Fairytale Drive, and what happened last year, because if I don't it'll all be forgotten, like the hot weather we had ... remember that?

Fairytale Drive wasn't really called that, of course. Its proper name was Farradale Drive and all it had was seven detached houses standing in a circle. Between no. 10 and no. 12 there was a little passageway, which we called The Ginnel, leading into Norsten Road where I live. Our houses are semis, but I can see no. 12 from my bedroom window. All the houses on Fairytale Drive have huge gardens, and fortunately most of them have some sort of gap in their fences that we could get through, which made things much easier for us last summer.

I suppose we were a gang, even though there were only three of us. I'm the only one left, now that Midge and Toby have gone, and I miss them. Part of telling you about this is a way of remembering them, and part is a sort of confession, even though I'm not sure that we did anything wrong.

Is it wrong to make things up? I don't mean lying or telling untruths to get something out of someone, or cheat them. I mean, inventing things, telling stories, recounting fantasies ... is that dangerous? I think it is, a bit. I think if you tell things well enough, and make people believe them, they're halfway to coming true. Midge was amazing. She never doubted any of her own stories, and she'd look you straight in the face and her eyes ... it was impossible not to be almost swallowed up in her pale grey eyes, and you would watch her mouth as it said the most impossible things, and half of you would want to laugh and say: 'Come off it, Midge,' and the other half of you couldn't help believing.

She looked very strange too. She was older than her brother Toby, who was in my class. She was nearly twelve, I think. Once I asked her how old she was and she just answered:

'As old as the hills, Ian. Maybe older.'

That was exactly the daft sort of stuff she said all the time, only you never told her it was daft, and you never even thought it was, not while you were listening. She was skinny and tall and freckled, with those eyes I've mentioned, and red hair. Midge's hair was the reddest I've ever seen, and it hung down her back in two long plaits that looked dead old-fashioned.

I know a lot about girls. I've got five girl cousins, and I don't care if I *am* being sexist when I say they spend huge amounts of time and effort and talk on what they look like. Midge was different. She never seemed to care, and she always looked the same in old T-shirts and faded denim shorts. Toby was short and plumpish and dark. His hair was curly. Midge used to say:

'I don't look like Toby because I'm a changeling. I've always known *they're* not my real parents. Didn't you know that, Ian, about people with red hair? They're very often changelings.'

I didn't say anything. Well, what could I say? That Midge's mother looked just like her, only older? Midge would probably have kicked me. People often pretend they're not really their parents' children. I'd done it for a bit. When I was about seven, I had this pretend game that a Prince had given me to my mum and dad to take care of, but I always knew it *was* a pretend game and I stopped playing it after a while.

The Fairytale Drive thing happened because there

wasn't enough to do last summer, and it was so hot that we couldn't be bothered to go to the park, and getting the bus into town was sticky and horrible and we couldn't face it. We went swimming a lot, and that was great, but we could only go when someone felt like taking us in the car, because the pool was so far away.

This left hours and hours for mooching around in. Midge, because she was older, was the one in charge, and she was always the one who decided what we did. She was the one who told us about Fairytale Drive.

We were sitting on the low wall outside no. 18, in the shade of a big tree, and Midge said:

'Look at no. 12. Do you know who lives there?'

'It's Mrs Gardener,' said Toby. 'I know her. She's got a pointy nose and grey hair.'

'She's got two grown-up daughters,' I said. 'I've seen them. One is fat and has sticky-out teeth.'

'And the other is skinny and spotty,' said Toby.

'Have you ever seen the third daughter?' Midge asked. 'The youngest? She's very pretty.'

'I've never seen a pretty one,' I said. 'Are you sure, Midge?'

'Sure as eggs is eggs,' said Midge. 'You never see her because she does all the housework. She's Cinderella.'

'What ever are you talking about?' I asked. 'I think the heat's melted your brains.'

Midge shook her head, and then she told us all about Fairytale Drive. She went from house to house. That fat man in no. 10, with the very pink face and the flattened nose was actually the third Little Pig. Hadn't we seen the hairy workman hanging around outside his house? Well, that was the Wolf, of course. All those students in no. 14 … didn't we think it odd that there were so many young men and only one woman in that house? Hadn't we noticed her dark, dark hair and very pale skin? Obviously, she was Snow White.

'It stands to reason,' was the way Midge put it. On and on she went, talking and talking while the afternoon burned on, and as she spoke, we got caught up in her tales and never noticed the heat. That old bearded chap in no. 16, for instance, had just got married to a woman who was *much* younger than he was ... his beard *did* have a definitely blueish tinge to it, Midge said. Didn't we think so? Didn't we think he looked like the type who could easily have a few ex-wives hidden away in a locked room? We did. We did, at least while Midge was telling her stories.

A van pulled up as we sat on the wall that day.

'See that?' said Midge. ' "MacIntosh Fish. Fresh daily." That's what it says,' she nodded. A small man got out of the van and walked up to the front door. 'That's Mr MacIntosh,' Midge whispered. 'Wait till you see his wife. She bosses him around. She's enormous and nags him all the time. I've heard her. Nothing's good enough for her. He found a Magic Fish once, you know. It grants his wishes. The MacIntoshes won't stay in Fairytale Drive long. She's going to get him to wish for a palace soon, and then they'll be off, you'll see.'

That's how the game began, and we played it all summer: pretending that every house in the Drive belonged not to ordinary people, but to characters from stories. The young girl we sometimes saw at the highest window of no. 20 was Rapunzel, naturally, and her mother was the witch. So it went on. All summer long we crept in and out of people's gardens and spied on them. I'm ashamed of it now. I don't think it's a nice thing to do: go looking into people's windows, but Midge had made it all right. She'd made it seem no worse than wandering through a sort of theme-park.

'We're not touching anything,' she used to say. 'We're doing no harm.'

I don't think we *were* doing any harm, but there's something dishonest about it, isn't there? Something creepy about people not knowing that you're looking at them. I suppose we would have got fed up with the game quite quickly, but the strange thing was that the more we looked, the more real evidence we seemed to be collecting that our neighbours were indeed exactly who Midge had told us they were.

We saw Cinderella down on her hands and knees scrubbing the floor as if Hoovers and polishers hadn't been invented. We found the hairy workman with his big, hairy hands pressed up against Mr Pig's French windows, and although we never heard him say: 'Little Pig, little Pig, let me come in!' he looked as though he might, at any moment. Once, we looked into Snow White's front window, and couldn't see any of the young men anywhere. An old woman, sitting at the dining-room table was showing her a whole lot of jewellery.

'And look!' Midge whispered. 'There's the Magic Comb. Can you see it?' We nodded, and ran away to the safety of the road.

So it went on. A 'For Sale' sign appeared outside the MacIntosh house

'I expect the Magic Fish has found them a palace,' said Midge, and we believed her. Everything fitted. Everything worked. We had our own living peep-show going on around us all day long.

But it wasn't Midge who found the Gingerbread House. I did that. It was on the corner of Fairytale Drive and the main road, and I don't know why Midge left it out of our games. It's true that you could hardly see it from any-where in the Drive, and that was because there were trees and huge shrubs growing right up to the doors and windows. My mum had a thing about the house. Every time we passed it, she'd mutter something about Mrs Ellison being a mole.

'How can anyone live without light like that?' she'd say. 'Those branches cover up all the downstairs windows.'

'Do you know her?' I asked.

'Not really,' she said. 'I know of her. She fosters children who need a home for a short time, when their own parents find it hard to look after them for some reason.'

Even though I knew about the fostering, I never mentioned it to Midge and Toby, on the afternoon when we saw two small children arriving at the house sur-rounded by trees. They stood for a couple of seconds in the road, looking lost and white-faced and I couldn't help what happened next. They looked just like Hansel and Gretel, so I said:

'They're Hansel and Gretel, aren't they, Midge, and that's the Gingerbread House.' She stared at them for a while, and then turned to me and smiled. Midge didn't smile very often, but when she did you felt that you'd been given a kind of present.

'Yes, Ian,' she said. 'Yes.' And then she murmured: 'It was clever of you to spot the house in the forest. I've known it's a witch's house for some time. I've seen the kids. They come and they're skinny and miserable, and then they get plumper and much happier and then they disappear.' She stared at me. 'I didn't mention it because Toby gets nightmares, but *you* know, Ian, don't you … what happens to those children?'

I nodded and shivered, even though the sun was shining. Half of me, most of me, was thinking: what a load of rubbish! Of course the children get plump. Mrs Ellison is kind and feeds them well and looks after them properly. *Of course* they disappear. They're only being fostered for a while, until their real parents or adoptive parents can look after them again. Of course they don't stay long. Of course new children keep coming. There was a perfectly normal explanation for everything. I should have said so to Midge, but I didn't. I revelled in the idea of a witch living so close to us, and more than any of the other inhabitants of Fairytale Drive, I believed in Hansel and Gretel. I lay in bed and thought about that oven, and I couldn't get the idea of Hansel in his cage out of my dreams.

We were sitting on the wall one day, bored with all the other houses, and moaning about not being able to get into Mrs Ellison's garden, which Midge called 'The Forest.' The gate was locked (why?); the fence was high and there were no gaps to slip through.

'There's Gretel,' Midge said suddenly. 'Let's talk to her.'

'No,' I cried, thinking: that's against the rules. I think I was frightened that our fairytales might vanish into thin air if we ever actually talked to anyone. I was too late. Midge had gone up to the gate and was talking to the little girl.

'Hello,' she said. 'What's your name?'

'Greta,' said the girl. A cloud appeared in the sky and covered up the sun, and in the shade of the trees we were almost in darkness.

'How old are you?'

'Five.'

'Where's your brother?'

'Inside,' said the little girl. Greta.

'Why doesn't he come out and play?' Midge asked.

'He can't,' said Greta.

'Why not?'

'Mrs Ellison said so. He's tired.'

'Do you like it here?' Midge said.

'Yes,' said Greta. Then: 'I want my Mummy.'

'Is Mrs Ellison kind to you?' I asked.

Greta nodded. 'She makes cakes. I like cakes. She lets me help her.'

The side door of the Gingerbread House opened, and there was Mrs Ellison herself. She didn't look a bit like a witch. She looked like a lovely granny, the kind you see on TV advertisements.

'Come in now, Greta,' she smiled, and she waved at us. 'Hello, children! It's time for Greta's supper.'

The little girl turned and walked to where Mrs Ellison was standing.

'Look!' Midge whispered. 'She's frightened. She doesn't want to go ...'

I looked at Midge. Her grey eyes were burning, and her face was quite white. She turned to me and Toby.

'We must tell someone,' she said. 'I'm really scared. We must tell your mum, Ian.' So we did. We went to my house and told her. Not everything of course. We didn't mention Fairytale Drive, or Hansel and Gretel. My mum would have thought we were mad. All we said was we thought the little girl looked frightened, and was she sure Mrs Ellison wasn't mistreating her in some way. My mum's got as many faults as anyone else's mother, but she *does* listen, and she takes what you say seriously. She listened, and she told us all about Mrs Ellison, and she managed to cheer me up. Midge and Toby went home, so I don't know how they felt. I went to bed feeling happy, and knowing that tonight I wouldn't dream of a skinny boy locked up in a metal cage.

The fire engines woke me up. I ran to the window and the whole sky was red. Even in the house, the smell of burning nearly choked us. My parents were up, and in their dressing-gowns. Someone was shouting. I'd never seen a real fire before, and I wanted to go out and have a look, but my mother wouldn't let me.

'Whose house is it?' I asked. 'Do you know whose house it is?' My mum looked as if she'd been crying.

'It's Mrs Ellison's,' she said. I said nothing. I just looked out of the window at the night that was suddenly no longer dark. I couldn't get rid of the pictures in my mind: pictures of Mrs Ellison being pushed into her own oven. Stop! I told myself. She's probably got a modern electric cooker. Stop this nonsense ... it's a game. It's only a game.

In the end, there was nothing else to see, and I went to bed. The last thought I had before I fell asleep was to wonder whether Midge and Toby had seen the fire. They must have done. The whole street must have seen it.

The day after the fire, Mum told me that poor Mrs Ellison had died.

'Are the children all right?' I asked.

'Yes,' said Mum. 'Thank God. They've gone back to their parents. It must have been terrible for them.'

I sat on the wall that afternoon with Midge and Toby and told them what my mum had said. Toby was silent. Midge looked at the burned-out, blackened shell of the Gingerbread House and said only:

'It stands to reason.'

We never played the Fairytale Drive game again. Midge and Toby left a couple of weeks later. Their dad had found a job in Saudi Arabia and their house was up for sale.

In the middle of October, someone bought the ruins of the Gingerbread House, and its garden. The trees were cut down. Bulldozers came and started clearing away what was left of the building. The men on the bulldozers were really nice, and let me potter about among the broken bricks and rubble. I've never told anyone about what I found. I put the first two in my trouser pockets, and next day, when I went back, I made sure to take a carrier bag for the others. There were sixteen altogether, scorched, charred to blackness, and scattered all over the place by the builders: children's shoes. Very small children's shoes. Maybe Mrs Ellison's foster children had left them behind when they went home. Or maybe not. I know which story Midge would have believed. One day when Mum was out, I dug a hole in the garden and buried the shoes in it, and said a prayer over them. Just in case.

the magic
fruit machine

hazel townson

G ran thought Bernie and Kate deserved a treat. She took them off to a seaside hotel for a holiday. There was only one thing wrong with the hotel. It had a fruit machine in the hall.

Bernie fell instantly in love with that fruit machine. He had spotted it the minute they arrived. Even while Gran was busy checking in, he dropped ten pence into the slot, pulled the lever – and won a pound! It was the best thing that had happened to him for ages.

After that, Bernie was hooked. He played that machine as often as he could when nobody was about. It was great fun, made even more exciting by the thrill of risking discovery.

By the end of two days that machine had gobbled up every penny of Bernie's holiday money.

Gran was shocked when she found out.

'I wish I'd noticed the wretched thing when we first arrived,' she said guiltily. 'Don't go near it again! Can't you see that you never win on those things?'

'I won a whole pound the first day,' protested Bernie.

'Yes, and promptly lost it again. The only people who end up with a profit are the ones who own the machines.'

Bernie thought Gran was mistaken. Anyway, all his holiday money was in that machine and he was determined to get it back. He borrowed a pound from a boy staying in the hotel, then another, and another. He meant to pay it back as soon as he won, of course. But he didn't win, and after a while the boy complained to Gran.

Gran was furious. She settled the debt, but rang up

Bernie's dad and asked him to come at once and take him home. He had to learn not to disobey.

Kate was upset. She was fond of Bernie and felt worried about him. Was he going to turn into a reckless gambler who would always be in debt? She decided to find out from Gypsy Gina, the fortune-teller on the pier.

LET ME MAKE YOUR FUTURE CRYSTAL CLEAR!

read the sign on Gina's booth.

She listened carefully to Kate's story. Then, to Kate's amazement, she offered a cure. She could make Bernie stop gambling for ever.

'How much will it cost? I haven't much money,' admitted Kate.

The gypsy thought for a minute, then named a figure, which turned out to be exactly the amount of money Kate had left from her holiday allowance. The gypsy must have known – but how? Such uncanny power convinced Kate that the woman could really help.

Gypsy Gina took Kate's money, then wrote down her address and told her that a parcel would arrive for Bernie on the day that Kate went home. That parcel would definitely cure his gambling.

A parcel? This was not what Kate had expected. Had she been tricked after all? Suppose no parcel ever turned up?

Yet on the very day she got home, a strange-looking parcel did arrive for Bernie – a parcel as big as a microwave oven.

At first he was suspicious. Parcels were for birthdays and Christmas, and today was just an ordinary day. He opened the parcel carefully – then suddenly whooped for joy. In it was a fruit-machine, a smaller model of the one in the hotel. It was the best present anyone could have sent.

There was no note, but Bernie guessed it must have come from his repentant dad as a consolation for the loss of half that holiday.

Kate was shocked. She knew the history of the parcel, but how could a fruit machine cure anyone of gambling? She had been tricked by the gypsy after all.

Bernie added insult to injury by asking Kate to lend him ten pence so that he could try out the machine. Kate almost refused, then she realised that it was the only way to discover the truth. Perhaps this machine was not what it seemed and the gypsy was trying to help after all.

Kate handed over the money and Bernie fed the coin into the machine. As soon as he pulled the lever there was an instant whirring sound followed by a rumbling, clattering noise as a huge cascade of coins poured into the miniature metal cup and spilled over on to the carpet! Bernie had won the jackpot first go!

The children stared in surprise. Bernie fed in another coin and the same thing happened! A second jackpot spilled all over the floor.

This was too much for Kate. Some cure this was going to be! 'Our folks will go mad!' she cried. 'Especially Gran. We've got to hide this thing before anybody sees it.'

'But I thought dad sent it ...' began Bernie, already enthusiastically feeding in a third coin.

Kate snatched his hand away. 'No, he didn't! It's all a big mistake. Quick! You'll have to help me move it.'

She scooped the scattered coins into a scarf, tied the ends together and placed it on top of the machine. Then they each took one end of the fruit machine and started upstairs.

'In here!' Kate gestured towards her bedroom.

But Bernie wasn't having that.

'It's my present. I want it in MY room!'

There was no time to argue.

'Oh, all right, but DON'T YOU DARE TOUCH IT!'

Before long, Bernie was left alone with his wonderful present. It was his, and he'd jolly well do what he liked with it. He grabbed the lever defiantly and pulled as if his life depended on it.

He won again, as much money as before!

Now Bernie was confused as well as elated, for surely there shouldn't be all these jackpots one after another? It wasn't good for business. He was quite prepared to lose a good few coins. Yet the next pull on the lever was just as successful. Those wonderful coins came tumbling out again – and again! Jackpot after jackpot! It was impossible to lose!

Common sense told him there must be a limit, of course. The machine would only hold a certain number of coins. Once he had won them all, there would be no more. He tried to guess how much money the machine might hold. Fifty pounds? A hundred? More?

He decided that he had better not stop until he had emptied the machine, just in case it was taken away from him. But the money kept on flowing until it was obvious that there was far more on the floor than would fit into the machine.

Now, there was a puzzle!

Perhaps the machine was magic? Perhaps there really WAS no end to the flow of money? Bernie remembered a fairy tale he had once read about a pot of soup that kept on refilling whenever it was emptied. Maybe his machine was like that! He began to picture himself growing richer by the minute. He might even end up a millionaire!

Soon the situation was getting out of control. Coins flew thick and fast. No longer did they simply spill on to the floor. They began to shoot up into the air and to fly in all directions. They bounced off the walls and furniture. They whizzed around the room like maddened bees. They zoomed at the windows, settled in swarms on the bed and filled the room with an ominous humming noise.

Bernie began to feel frightened. That ought to have stopped him working the machine, but it didn't. He wanted to stop by this time, yet his hand seemed bewitched. He could no longer tear it away from the fateful lever. He just kept on pulling and pulling, while the humming grew a hundred times worse. At last he had to shout for help, no longer caring who heard him.

Luckily for him, it was Kate who came rushing to the bedroom door.

'I thought I told you not to touch that machine? For goodness' sake stop pulling that lever!'

'I CAN'T stop!' yelled Bernie.

'Don't be silly; of course you can! You HAVE to!' Kate began fighting her way through the deep drifts of coins towards Bernie.

'I can't Kate, honest! My hand's stuck to this lever.'

Kate tried to snatch her brother's hand away but it was impossible. Grasping Bernie by the wrist, she tugged and tugged but could not move his hand. Something was holding it tighter than superglue. At last, on the verge of despair, Kate spotted a bright red button on the back of the machine that read: EMERGENCY STOP. Thankful, she pressed the button. The machine stopped immediately, and Bernie's hand fell free.

What a relief!

At the same moment the coins ceased flying around the room and settled themselves into little heaps all over the furniture and the floor. There was a sudden, wonderful silence.

Now, when it was almost too late, Kate was beginning

to see what the fortune-teller must have intended. Bernie had been given a serious fright, and this was bound to be false money anyway. No doubt Bernie WOULD be cured now, but it was a terrible way for it to happen.

'We have to get rid of this thing as fast as we can,' Kate announced in a shaky voice. But that was too much for Bernie. In spite of his shock, he was already determined to try the machine again. He was obsessed. He would keep on until he was sure there was no money left in it.

'I'll wear a glove this time,' he decided. 'Then my hand won't stick to the lever. It'll be all right, you'll see.'

Kate was shocked to the core. What was happening to Bernie? Yet an even worse shock was in store. Even as the children stood there arguing, the heaps of fallen coins began to turn to water. First they formed little pools, like melting ice-cubes. Then the pools spread out to touch one another. Soon those pools began to heave and deepen until they were lapping and slapping against the walls of the room like menacing tidal waves.

At last the whole room was awash. Even the bedding and furniture rose to the occasion and took to floating alongside the books, pyjamas, toys, even the posters from the walls. The children were swept off their feet as the water level rose alarmingly. With a cry of dismay, Bernie floundered against the machine, banged his head on it and began to sink beneath the water. Bernie could not swim!

Kate struggled frantically towards him and just managed to grab him by the collar and heave him to the door. Bernie's eyes were closed and he seemed to be unconscious. Panting and spluttering, Kate wrenched the door open and a great cascade of water swept the pair of them down the stairs.

Hours later, when Bernie had been taken to hospital,

the fire chief explained that a storage tank had burst in the loft above Bernie's bedroom, but Kate knew better. That machine was bewitched and until they got rid of it anything could happen.

As soon as the firemen had departed she ran back to Bernie's bedroom to look for the machine. But it had disappeared! There was no sign of it anywhere. Perhaps it had turned to water too.

Kate searched all over that damp and ruined room, but all she found was a single tenpenny coin trapped behind the radiator.

As for Bernie, that knock on the head seemed to have caused him some slight loss of memory. He never mentioned the fruit machine again. Whenever Kate dropped hints about it, he just looked completely blank. It was as if that wicked machine had never existed.

Next summer, when they all returned to the seaside, Kate went in search of Gypsy Gina but she was nowhere to be found. Even her booth had disappeared. So the mystery of the magic fruit machine was never solved.

babblish

richard brassey

'**W**e're getting a chimpanzee at the lab,' said Tom's mother. 'If you want to you can help look after it.'

'Are you kidding?' yelled Tom. 'Of course I want to.'

Tom's mother, Dr Babble, was a scientist with big plans. For some time she had been busy inventing a new language which would be so easy that everybody in the world could learn it after only a few lessons.

'I hope it'll be easier than French,' groaned Tom. He'd just started this at school and was finding it pretty hard.

His mother told him that all through history wars had started because people had not understood each other properly.

'Men and women who speak different languages or have funny accents are often laughed at, picked on or even killed,' she said. 'If everybody speaks Babblish' – as her new language was to be called – 'the bullies of the world will have one less reason to pick on others.'

People have tried to invent a perfect language before, but never with the help of such powerful computers as Dr Babble had. Her laboratory was right next door to their house and Tom loved to wander down the rows and rows of processors, each with thousands of megabytes of memory.

For almost two years men and women had come from all over the world to teach the computers to speak their different languages. On days when he was not at school, Tom got quite used to sitting down to lunch with ten or more people who could not understand anything each other said. Even the simplest things took hours of explaining.

'Salt, please,' he once asked a tall man next to him. 'Salt,' it turned out, was the rudest word you could possibly say in this man's language. His mother had to spend half an hour calming the man down before he would return to the table. Tom began to understand how speaking different languages might indeed have started wars.

On another occasion a woman of a hundred and two arrived from South America. His mother was extremely excited because she was the last person in the world who knew how to speak a certain ancient language. The old lady taught one of the computers everything she could remember.

'Can you imagine,' said Tom's mother. 'If it were not for computer number 429, her language would die with her.'

The language that appealed most to Tom was the African Bushman's click language. To speak this you have to click your tongue on the roof of your mouth every so often. His mother had explained to him that the click was like one of the hard letters in the alphabet such as 't' or 'p' or 'k'. Tom enjoyed making the sound so much that for quite some time he would add a click or two in the middle of nearly everything he said.

At last the great day came.

'Finished!' announced his mother. 'We've collected nearly six thousand languages. So far as we know that's as many as there are in the world.' By tapping a few keys on her keyboard she joined all the computers together in such a way that they could search and search to find words and sentences which would be easy for everybody in the world to understand. For two days and two nights the computers made little grating noises. Sometimes they would all grate at once and the noise was deafening. Sometimes they would all go quiet as though pausing for thought. Then one of them would start up again and another would join in and you never knew if they'd all join in each time or just as suddenly go quiet. The whole while his mother and her assistants, Jane and Simon, sat gazing at their monitors and, every so often, hammering frantically on their keyboards.

Tom got quite used to putting himself to bed and making his own meals in the microwave.

Then, on the morning of the third day, his mother came racing in trailing a long roll of computer printout.

'Tom, come quick!' she shouted breathlessly.

Tom dropped the breakfast he had carefully prepared of ice cream, a chocolate bar and a packet of crisps, and raced after her to the lab. They all gathered around the main computer's voice synthesiser.

'Blah snig fliggo (click),' said the computer in its flat mechanical voice.

'Blah (click) sniggo flig,' answered Dr Babble.

'Blog!' said the computer firmly, and everybody clapped and cheered and congratulated Dr Babble. They had just had their first conversation in Babblish.

The next thing was to persuade everybody in the world to speak the newly invented language. This was where the chimp came in. Chimpanzees are our nearest animal cousins, but are not quite as clever as we are. Tom's mother felt certain that if she could teach a chimpanzee Babblish, it would be easy to persuade people to learn it. A huge advertising campaign was planned with the slogan 'Babblish – so simple a chimp can speak it!'

'We've found a chimp,' said Tom's mother one day. 'It's a little girl chimp. She's only three years old so she'll need lots of love and attention.'

'Isn't that too young to take her away from her mother?' said Tom.

'You're right,' answered his mother. 'I've been very careful about that. This little one was born in a zoo. Chimp mothers in zoos often don't know how to look after their babies properly and reject them. Mothering is something that has to be taught. If the chimps were born in zoos themselves or kidnapped from the wild and didn't know their own mothers, they never learn how, so the zookeepers have to look after their babies. Our little one is an orphan. I think we can give her a much nicer home than she would have in a zoo, don't you? Besides, she will probably become quite famous as the first chimp to speak Babblish.'

Of course, if Tom were to help with teaching the chimp, he would have to learn Babblish too.

'It won't be like learning French,' his mother promised, and it did turn out to be very easy. Hardly any of the words had more than four letters and some of them sounded so silly they made him laugh. Best of all, the computers had decided that the Bushman's click made a perfect way of saying 'yes'.

His mother gave him a Babblish lesson each day after school.

'When people speak,' she explained, 'they use their hands and faces to say things just as much as their voices. But these gestures and expressions are different all over the world. So we've made a particular face or sign to go with every Babblish word. For instance, whenever you make the click with your mouth, you simply click your finger and thumb at the same time.'

'Like this?' clicked Tom. The two clicks together made a satisfying noise that over the next few days he found himself saying 'yes' a lot more often than he meant to. Tom and his mother and Jane and Simon took to speaking Babblish nearly all the time.

Tom's mother had already built a large, comfortable cage at the laboratory. It was specially heated with all sorts of climbing frames and swings and an outside area so the chimp could go out in fine weather. There was even a tree growing in it.

'We want her to be happy,' said Tom's mother. 'Chimps get bored just like us if they have nothing to do. By the way, Sir Sidney thinks she should be called Babs.'

Sir Sydney Boss, chairman of the board of Babbletec, was not a man to be argued with. Babbletec was the company which had been set up to make sure that everybody in the world would want to learn Babblish, thus making it a more peaceful place. The board were the people who paid for everything, including Tom's mother's laboratory. They were mostly very rich already and they planned to become a great deal richer when Babblish caught on. There are six billion people in the world and they would all need to buy the *Teach Yourself Babblish* book which Tom's mother was writing, not to mention the tape, the video and the CD Rom.

The day the chimp was due to arrive, Tom waited impatiently until at last a white van drove in at the gate. A tall man with a thin moustache got out of the driver's seat, carrying a folder of papers for Dr Babble to sign. This seemed to take an age, but eventually the man pulled a small box roughly from the back of the van and Tom's mother led the way into the new chimp house.

'Blimey!' said the man, dropping the box carelessly on the floor and looking around. 'What's this – Buckingham Palace? I'll be off then,' he added without waiting for a reply. A few seconds later they heard the van door slam and the engine started up.

Tom and his mother stood looking at each other. They

had expected the man would at least take the chimp out and introduce them.

'Can I open the box?' whispered Tom.

'Be careful,' whispered his mother.

Two eyes, blinking in the bright light, and a row of white teeth greeted Tom as he pulled back the lid. Gingerly, and speaking in what he hoped was a soothing voice, he reached in for the dark hairy little body. Immediately the chimp began to screech. The noise was so earsplitting that Tom very nearly dropped her, but he kept a firm hold, and, pulling her up into his arms, gave her a hug. The little chimp stopped shrieking. Her arms shot around his neck, one hand entwining itself in his hair, where the fingers started a gentle stroking movement.

Tom's mother came over. 'Hello Babs,' she said. The chimp gazed at her for a second, then buried her face in Tom's neck, sucking furiously at the thumb on her other hand. Every so often a small sob racked her body.

The little chimp stayed like this for the rest of the day. As soon as anybody showed the slightest sign of trying to take her away from Tom, she would start screeching until they moved away. Although this was inconvenient for Tom, who began wanting to go to the bathroom around the middle of the afternoon, he couldn't help being proud that she felt safe in his arms. His mother had prepared a bottle of milk, which at first the little chimp would not even look at, but eventually Tom was able to place a small drop on her tongue. Suddenly she seemed to realise how hungry she was. She grabbed the bottle and began sucking desperately. The last drop of milk had hardly gone before her eyes closed and the bottle fell from her hand.

By this time Tom was hopping from foot to foot. As gently as he could, he undid the other hand which was still gripping his hair and placed the little creature on her new bed. Her arms and legs suddenly shot out. Tom was certain she was going to wake up, but instead she made a snuffling noise and settled down. His mother laid a blanket over her and they both stood looking for a moment at the puckered little face. The blanket moved up and down in the peaceful rhythm of sleep.

'Poor little thing. She must have been exhausted,' said Tom's mother. Tom did not answer. He was halfway to the bathroom. He was bursting.

Next morning Tom was up as soon as it was light and found his mother awake too. She seemed almost as anxious as he to get over to the lab and say 'good morning' to the new arrival.

They found her sitting on a bar beside her bed, staring into space.

'Why's she rocking from side to side?' asked Tom softly.

'It's because she's upset. People do the same thing.' Tom's mother unlocked the door and Tom stepped in, trying not to alarm her with any sudden movement. The little chimp seemed hardly to notice him until he got close and held out his hand. Then her lips reached forward in a pout and began softly exploring his out-stretched fingers. It was a funny tickly feeling. She stared deeply into his eyes as though saying 'Can I trust you?' Tom moved a little closer. Her arm came out and with one movement she locked herself into the same tight hug around his neck as on the day before.

It was like this every day. Whenever Tom was with her, she spent the whole time with her arms locked around his neck. When he was not there, she sat rocking from side to side and screeching if anybody else came near.

The programme for teaching Babblish to Babs had been carefully worked out and after a couple of weeks Tom's mother said it was time to begin. Babs was spending less time hugging Tom, and even showed signs of wanting to play as long as he was close by. Tom began to speak and sign to her in Babblish.

Although chimpanzees can learn to understand spoken language, if Babs were ever to 'speak' Babblish herself it would have to be with the signs. Chimps' mouths are different from ours and they cannot literally speak.

When Tom's mother or Simon or Jane came into the cage, Babs would immediately run to Tom and fling her arms around him, refusing to move until they left. If they came in when Tom was not there, Babs would simply ignore them by sitting rocking and staring into space. Tom's class from school came and the visit was a disaster. She spent the whole time hugging tight to Tom and refused to look up once.

'I thought chimps were meant to be fun,' he heard one of his classmates say.

Tom's mother was worried. Sir Sydney and the board were getting impatient.

'If she doesn't cooperate soon, we'll have to find another chimp. It's very sad,' she said, 'but I don't know what else we can do.'

Tom couldn't help himself. He burst into tears.

'We can't get rid of Babs,' he sobbed. 'I'm sure she'll learn.' And it was true. He knew that each day Babs understood more and more of what he said to her, yet it was almost as if she was pretending not to. 'I know she's learning. Just give her a chance.'

'I don't want to get rid of her any more than you do, Tom,' said his mother. 'Maybe she *will* talk to you but she just screams when any of us go near her. What if we put a video camera in her cage? That way you can turn it on whenever you go in so we can watch the recordings later and see if she starts to talk when she's alone with you.'

Months went by. Everyone got pretty bored with watching videos where Babs showed no sign of learning Babblish at all. Tom himself felt sure that Babs understood what he said. The way her dark brown eyes gazed into his when he spoke told him quite plainly that she did. And yet he could never prove it. It was just a feeling he had.

'Tom,' said Dr Babble one day, 'we've had Babs a long time now. Sir Sydney and the board are insisting that we get another chimp. They won't give me the money to build another cage and there's nowhere else for Babs to live. She must have something wrong with her. Her behaviour isn't normal, so we can't risk putting the other chimp in with her. You're so good with chimps, you could look after the new one, but Babs will have to go. There's a man coming tomorrow who may be able to give her a home. He runs a sanctuary where she could live with other chimps. She wouldn't be far away and you could visit.'

'But you promised. You promised,' shouted Tom, rushing out of the room. He went straight to Babs's cage. The little chimp looked up, startled, as he slammed the door and sat down next to her.

'Please Babs, you must start to speak Babblish or they'll send you away. Please.' The Babblish word for "please" is 'fav'. 'Fav,' he sobbed, 'fav.' And he pulled his cupped hand towards himself in the sign which also means 'please'.

Tom could hardly see Babs through his tears, but he suddenly became aware that the little chimp was moving her arms and hands in a way he had never seen her do before. She was replying to him in Babblish signs. Once she had started, the words and sentences seemed to tumble out of her. Tom hardly dared move, but every so often he signed back to show he was listening and understood. She signed fluently in perfect Babblish. The only sign that gave her any trouble was the click because her thumb was so much smaller than a human thumb.

It was dark when Babs made her last signs. 'I'm tired. I want to sleep.' He watched her curl up under the blanket until he could tell by her breathing that she was sleeping. He felt stunned as he crept quietly from the cage. While the little chimp spoke he had thought of nothing else. Now he realised what this meant. They would not have to give Babs away. She spoke Babblish better than his mother could ever have hoped.

'She can speak! She can speak!' he yelled as he ran into his mother's office. 'Come quickly. She's asleep now but it'll all be on the video. She told me so many things.' His mother had been holding a meeting with Simon and Jane and the whole startled group jumped up and rushed directly to Babs's cage. Babs was still curled up fast asleep. Simon quickly ran over to rewind the tape.

'That's strange,' he said. 'Did you rewind this, Tom?'

With an immediate sinking feeling, Tom realised he had forgotten to switch on the video. He looked from one disbelieving face to the next.

'It's true. It's true. She can speak,' he pleaded. 'You'll see … tomorrow.'

But Babs did not speak Babblish the next day, so she would have to go away. Tom could not bear the thought of saying goodbye. He was hiding in his room when there was a knock at the door. It was the man who had come to collect her. He came in and sat down.

'Hello, Tom,' said the man. 'You've been doing a great job of looking after Babs, but I think she'd be happiest with other chimps, don't you? In the wild chimps always live in families. I've got a place where I look after a lot of chimps who have nowhere to go like Babs. There's plenty of space for them too.'

'But she'll miss me!' said Tom.

'She will, but she'll soon grow too strong for you to play with and you couldn't keep her as a pet any more. Babs has problems, you know. An adult human must have done something terrible to her before she came here. That's why she sits and rocks and screams if any adults try to touch her.'

But when the man went up to Babs himself, pouting at her and making little 'huh! huh!' noises, she immediately ran over to him and allowed him to pick her up.

'Wow!' said Tom. 'How did you do that?'

'I spend a lot of time with chimps,' he said. 'You can visit Babs whenever you like. She'll always remember you. Chimps remember just as well as humans, if not better.'

Tom felt that if Babs trusted this man, then so could he. So Babs went to live with the other chimps. She has grown into a happy member of her new family. Tom goes to see her often. He has never tried to speak Babblish to her again, but they always gaze into each other's eyes when they meet.

Tom's mother never did get another chimp. The months that Babs had spent with them made her think long and hard about whether it is right to try and force an animal to learn a human language against its will. It had never occurred to her that Babs might have had a good reason not to want to learn Babblish.

The day after Tom told his mother that Babs had spoken to him, in an effort to calm him, she had asked what Babs had said.

'She told me she was born in a hot country,' said Tom.

'She made the signs for "mother/man/stick/blood/not wake up". She told me about all the cruel people who brought her to this country. Mum, her mother was murdered by people in Africa. She was kidnapped and brought here!'

'That's nonsense,' said his mother. 'I know you're upset but there's no need to make things up. I have the papers in my office which prove that Babs was born in a zoo in Europe. They even give her mother's name. I don't want to hear any more about it.'

A few weeks later Dr Babble was reading the newspaper when she recognised a photograph of the tall man with the thin moustache who had delivered Babs. The story underneath said he had been arrested for bringing wild animals illegally from Africa and selling them to laboratories with false papers which said they had been born in zoos.

So it was a great relief when Sir Sydney Boss and the other board members suddenly changed their minds.

'We're going for the wrong image,' announced Sir Sydney. 'Our market research tells us that people think of chimpanzees as being clowns. We don't want to suggest that Babblish is a language for clowns! We've had a wonderful new idea. We're going to have a worldwide competition to find a perfect three-year-old child. The new slogan will be: 'Babblish – so simple a child can speak it.'

If you are wondering why you have never heard of Babblish, the reason is human nature. Most humans are lazy, and whether babies or chimps found it easy to learn made no difference. People could not be bothered with Babblish and were quite content to muddle on in their own native tongues.

But there is still a Babblish Club, of which Dr Babble is

Life President. It meets in a basement in West London every two months. If you stood outside during a meeting, you would be amazed at the amount of clicking going on inside.

These days most of Dr Babble's efforts go into the Babble Foundation which she started to save wild animals. She travels all over the world helping people of different countries to look after their wild animals and the places where they live. Simon and Jane still work with her. Tom loves helping his mother. For him it is a dream come true.

'Having so many different animals and people and languages in the world makes it a much more interesting place,' he said to his mother one day. 'It would be horrible if all the animals disappeared and there were just people left and they all spoke the same language.' Dr Babble could only agree.

unlucky for some

helen mccann

Don't walk on the cracks,' said Dave. 'It's unlucky.'
'You think everything is unlucky,' said Barry. 'Cracks in the pavement, walking under ladders, breaking mirrors – it's a lot of rubbish.'

Dave shook his head. 'It isn't,' he said. 'Mum spilled some salt yesterday and then this huge telephone bill came thumping through the letter box.'

'Oh,' said Barry. 'I don't suppose that could have anything to do with your mum, could it?'

Dave's mum was never off the phone. Dave grinned and said, 'Anyway, it isn't rubbish.'

'Hey, watch me!' said Barry. 'Race you to the end of the road. I bet I can hit every crack in the pavement from here to the corner.' And he started running.

'Barry!' Dave yelled after him.

But Barry wasn't listening. He was running, head down, looking for the cracks in the pavement. His feet hit the pavement as he ran – and every time they hit they landed on a crack.

He stopped at the corner, out of breath. 'Beat you,' he said as Dave came pelting up.

But Dave wasn't looking. 'There's been an accident,' he said.

Barry whirled round. There was an ambulance and a police car with its blue light flashing.

They saw two ambulance men lifting a stretcher into the ambulance. Then the police car revved its engine and drove away. Another car, a blue one, drove slowly after it.

A woman was standing on the pavement not far away.

'What happened?' said Barry.

'I don't know,' said the woman. 'One minute this man

was walking along the pavement. And the next minute he dashed out onto the road.' She looked worried. 'I hope he isn't badly hurt. The poor driver didn't stand a chance. I told the police that. The man just ran out into the road.'

The woman walked on, shaking her head.

Barry and Dave stood there a moment. Then Barry looked down. Something was lying there. It was a dull blue colour. Barry bent and picked it up. As his fingers touched it, he felt a shiver go through him. It felt cold – like some kind of stone. He put his other hand to his head.

'What's the matter?' said Dave.

'Nothing,' said Barry. 'I just felt sort of dizzy for a moment.'

'What's that you found?' asked Dave.

Barry opened his hand. 'I don't know,' he said. 'It looks really weird.'

Dave looked at the thing in Barry's hand. It was oval-shaped and it had funny markings on it. He put out his hand then drew it back.

'Throw it away,' he said.

'But I've only just found it,' said Barry. 'Maybe it belongs to that woman.'

'Or maybe it belongs to the man who was knocked down,' said Dave with a shiver. 'Throw it away. It feels unlucky. It gives me the creeps.'

'Everything gives you the creeps,' said Barry. 'It's like a beetle. Ugly thing, isn't it?' And he turned to cross the road.

Dave's hand shot out and grabbed him. 'Watch out,' he yelled as a bus whizzed past.

'Sorry,' said Barry. 'I didn't hear it coming.'

'Didn't hear a bus?' said Dave incredulously. 'Come on, let's get home before there's another accident.'

Barry looked at the blue beetle in his hand. 'Maybe

you're right about it being unlucky. Maybe it doesn't like being called ugly,' and he laughed.

'Don't joke,' said Dave. 'I've told you, that thing gives me the heebie jeebies.'

'Rubbish,' said Barry. 'It's only an old stone beetle.'

'Ugh!' said Barry's older sister that evening. 'It's horrible. Where did you get it?'

'I found it,' said Barry. 'And don't call it horrible. It doesn't like it.'

'Have you gone off your head?' said his sister.

'It was a joke,' said Barry.

His mum came into the kitchen. 'Turn the oven down, will you, Susan?' she said. 'I'm just going to take the washing in.' She looked at the beetle lying on the kitchen table. 'Where did you get that? It's horrible.' And she went out into the garden.

'Ow!' Susan yelled.

Barry turned round. Susan was holding her arm.

'What happened?' he said.

'That oven door,' said Susan. 'It swung open and caught my arm.'

There was a red burn mark on her arm.

'You should be more careful,' Barry said. 'I'll get the first aid box.'

'Get the first aid box, Barry,' said his mum, coming in the back door.

Barry turned, surprised. 'I was just going to,' he said. Then he stopped. 'What happened?' There was blood on his mum's forehead.

'The washing line snapped,' she said. 'It caught me just above the eye. Lucky it wasn't a bit lower.' Then she saw

Susan. 'What on earth happened to you?' she said.

'I burnt my arm,' Susan said.

Barry's mum shook her head. 'They say things come in threes, I wonder what's going to happen next. Now, where's that first aid box?'

Barry made a dive for the first aid box. He put it down on the table next to the beetle. Then he picked up the beetle. It felt cold in his hand. He put it in his pocket. Things happen in threes. That was what his mum said. Well, he thought, he had nearly been knocked down by a bus, Susan had burnt her arm and Mum had got a cut from the washing line. That was three things. Maybe their bad luck was over.

That night he put the beetle on his bedside table. It seemed to glow slightly in the dark. He turned over and went to sleep.

'You look tired,' his mum said next morning when he yawned for the third time.

'I had weird dreams,' said Barry. 'Funny, but I can't remember them – I just know they were weird.'

Barry found Dave coming out of the school library at break.

'Have you still got that thing?' Dave said.

'What thing?' said Barry. But he knew what Dave was talking about. The stone beetle was in his pocket. He could feel it. It seemed heavy for such a small thing.

'You know what,' said Dave.

Barry took the stone beetle out of his pocket. 'This?' he said, waving it in front of Dave's face.

Dave's hands came up and he pushed Barry away. 'Don't do that,' he said. He seemed really uptight.

'Relax,' said Barry. 'What are you so worried about?'

Dave pulled a book out of his jacket pocket. 'Look,' he said. 'I got this in the library.'

'What is it?' said Barry. *Ancient Egypt: Myths and Curses*, it said on the front cover.

'It's a scarab,' Dave said. He opened the book and found the page he was looking for.

'Your beetle,' he said. 'Look,' and he turned the book so that Barry could see.

Barry looked at the picture. It showed a dull blue beetle-shaped thing. It was his beetle. Or at least it looked just like it.

'It's a scarab,' Dave said again. There was an odd note in his voice.

Barry put his hand in his pocket and took out the stone beetle. Then he looked at the picture in the book.

'That's amazing,' he said. 'What does the book say about it?'

'It says a lot of this stuff was stolen from the pyramids,' said Dave.

'The pyramids?' Barry said. 'They're in Egypt.'

Dave nodded. 'They're tombs – you know, where they buried their kings thousands of years ago.'

'So?' said Barry.

'So, years ago people used to rob the tombs. These kings were buried with all kinds of gear – jewels and gold and stuff like that.'

'What are you getting at?' Barry said.

'Only that this book says that funny things happened to people who robbed the tombs.'

'What kind of funny things?' said Barry.

'Accidents,' said Dave.

'So you reckon this beetle came from one of these old tombs?' said Barry. 'Get a grip, Dave.' He looked at the object in his hand. 'What did you call it?'

'A scarab,' said Dave. 'I tell you, they're unlucky.'

'Well, I don't suppose this came all the way from ancient Egypt,' said Barry.

'What didn't come from ancient Egypt?' said a voice behind them. It was Mr Porter, their chemistry teacher. They liked Mr Porter.

'This,' said Barry, holding out his hand. The scarab lay on his palm. 'Dave says it's got a curse on it.'

'The curse of the mummy's tomb!' said Mr Porter. 'That old rubbish. I thought you had more sense than to fall for nonsense like that.'

'Not me,' said Barry. 'It's Dave that thinks there's a curse on it. He thinks somebody stole it from a pyramid.'

Mr Porter laughed. 'Looks more like it came out of a Christmas cracker,' he said. 'Nasty-looking thing, isn't it?'

The bell rang. 'Got to go,' said Mr Porter. 'See you!'

'See you!' said Barry. He felt better. Dave had been getting him worried. 'See,' he said to Dave. 'Mr Porter thinks that's all rubbish as well.'

'Maybe,' said Dave. 'But I still think you should throw it away.'

'No way,' said Barry. 'What if it really did come from a pyramid? Maybe it's worth a fortune.'

'Just tell me this then,' said Dave. 'How come you nearly got knocked down right after you picked it up?'

'That was nothing,' said Barry hastily.

'Has anything else happened?' asked Dave.

Barry thought of Susan's arm and his mum's forehead. That kind of thing could happen any time. 'Of course not,' he said. 'Don't be daft.'

'Are you sure?' said Dave.

Barry thought. Both Susan and his mum had said the

scarab was horrible. Rubbish, he said to himself. Dave was really putting the wind up him. And, besides, Mr Porter had said the scarab was a nasty-looking thing and nothing had happened to him.

'You're worrying about nothing,' he said. 'It's just you and your usual stuff. Cracks in the pavement. Friday the thirteenth. It's all a lot of rubbish. And don't tell me it's the scarab's fault if we get into trouble for being late for English. Come on, we're late. The bell went ages ago.'

He put the scarab back in his pocket. It lay there. It really was heavy.

It was half way through the next lesson when they heard the wail of an ambulance. Barry looked out of the window. The ambulance was turning into the school gates.

'What's up?' said Dave.

'Don't know,' said Barry.

Then he saw a figure being helped out to the ambulance. Barry's breath caught in his throat. It was Mr Porter. He had his hands up at his face.

'Settle down,' said Mrs Baker, the English teacher. Barry sat back down in his seat.

'That was Mr Porter,' he said.

Mrs Baker looked worried. 'Chemistry labs can be dangerous places,' she said. 'I hope he hasn't had an accident.'

Dave nudged Barry but Barry looked away. He didn't want to think about Mr Porter having an accident.

The classroom door opened and the headmaster came in.

'This class should be having chemistry next?' he said. Mrs Baker nodded.

The headmaster gave them a tight smile. 'No need to worry,' he said. 'Mr Porter had a little accident with an experiment, but he's going to be all right. And you can have a study period instead of chemistry.'

'Do you still think it's stupid?' Dave whispered to Barry.

Barry pursed his lips. Of course it was stupid. He didn't believe stuff like that – did he?

That night Barry put the scarab on his bedside table again. He looked at it before he fell asleep. Was he imagining things? Was it really glowing? Or was it just the light from the street lamp outside?

This time the dreams were even stranger. He seemed to be in a long dark tunnel. He felt as if he couldn't breathe. The air was heavy, choking him. Far ahead he thought he saw a light. It got brighter and brighter and the air got thicker and thicker. He woke up choking and coughing. His eyes were streaming. All around him the air was thick with smoke and beside him the scarab glowed. It really did glow. There were flames coming from his bedside lamp and from the pile of comics beside his bed. Suddenly Barry was wide awake. His bedroom was on fire!

He jumped out of bed and ran to the door, tugging at it. It wouldn't open. Tears streamed down his face. The smoke was getting thicker. He grabbed the duvet from his bed and threw it over the comics. Then he ran back to the door, hammering on it, pulling it, yelling.

It seemed ages before he heard his dad yelling on the other side of the door.

'There's a fire,' Barry shouted. He looked behind him. Smoke was beginning to creep round the edges of the duvet.

'Stand away from the door,' his dad yelled. 'It's stuck. I'm going to break it down.'

Barry stood back while his dad threw himself at the door. It crashed open and clean fresh air poured into the room. His mum was there, grabbing him. His dad was stamping on the duvet, beating out the flames.

The last thing Barry saw as he let his mum take him downstairs was the scarab, lying on his bedside table.

'It must have been a bad connection on the bedside lamp,' his dad said when he came downstairs. 'Are you all right, Barry?'

Barry nodded, but he didn't feel all right. And he didn't think the fire was due to the lamp. He swallowed hard. No, he didn't think Dave was talking rubbish any longer. He thought Dave was right.

'Can I sleep in your room tonight?' he said to his mum and dad.

'Well you can't sleep in yours, can you?' said his mum. 'He must be in shock,' she said to his dad.

But Barry wasn't in shock. He couldn't remember when he had last slept in his mum and dad's room – maybe when he was tiny. But he wasn't going to go anywhere near that scarab – not at night, not in the dark. Tomorrow, he thought. Tomorrow, he would get rid of it. But how?

Later, much later, Barry still lay awake on a camp bed in his mum and dad's room and wondered how he was going to get rid of it. It was almost morning before he fell asleep, but by then he knew what he was going to do with it.

'The canal,' he said to Dave next morning. 'I'll throw it in the canal. Then nobody else will ever find it.'

Dave looked relieved. 'I don't care what you do with it,' he said. 'Just get rid of it.'

'I'm going to,' said Barry. He had told Dave about the accidents to Susan and his mum, and about the fire.

'Mr Porter's going to be all right,' Dave said. His mum worked at the hospital, so she knew.

'What happened?' said Barry as they walked towards the canal.

'Acid,' said Dave. 'He knocked it over. Luckily he tripped and fell and most of it missed him.'

The scarab was in Barry's pocket, getting heavier and heavier. 'Come on,' he said. 'Let's hurry.' He could see the canal now.

They ran the last part of the way. There was nobody on the tow path. Barry felt a terrible sense of urgency. He had to get rid of the scarab. As he reached the bank, he put his hand in his pocket. The scarab was heavier than ever. It was a real effort to pull it out of his pocket. He looked down at it lying there in his hand. It seemed to weigh a ton.

'Throw it,' said Dave.

Barry lifted his arm – slowly.

'What's wrong?' shouted Dave. 'Throw it.'

The words seemed to come from far away. The scarab was so heavy, Barry could hardly bear the weight. He looked at the hand with the scarab in it. It was moving in an arc, but slowly, as if it was in slow motion.

He felt the scarab drag at his hand, drag at his arm. He tried to open his hand. It wouldn't open. The weight of the scarab was terrible now. It dragged his whole body forward – forward – then his feet were slipping, the bank was crumbling – and Barry was falling, falling into the canal.

The water closed over his head. Then he surfaced and there was Dave standing on the bank, yelling at him.

'Let it go!' he screamed. 'Open your hand. Let it go.'

Barry looked at his hand. It was closed around something but he couldn't remember what. Then, very slowly, with Dave yelling at him, he did as he was told. He opened his hand and turned it palm down. The scarab stayed where it was for a moment. Then it fell, tumbling over and over until it splashed into the water and disappeared.

Suddenly the world was clear again. Dave was yelling at him. The water was cold and he was scrabbling, swimming, scrambling up the bank. Dave hauled him out and he stood there on the tow path, dripping.

'The bank gave way,' Dave said to him.

Barry shook the water out of his eyes. He felt terrific. He felt as if somebody had lifted a huge weight off him.

'Oh, yeah?' he said. 'The bank gave way – just like that.'

'It's over now,' said Dave. 'Finished.'

Barry drew an enormous sigh of relief. 'It's down there among the mud and the weeds where nobody will ever be able to find it.' He looked at Dave. 'Come on, let's go home. And I promise I won't step on a crack in the pavement all the way.'

Later that day a little boy dipped his shrimping net into the canal. It came up covered in mud and weeds.

'No fish,' he said to his mum.

His mum dumped the mud out onto the bank. 'Come on,' she said. 'We'll get some ice-cream.'

The little boy took her hand. Then he turned back. There was something amongst the mud on the bank. Something blue and shaped like a beetle. He tugged his mum's hand but she only said, 'What about that ice-cream?'

The little boy forgot about the blue beetle lying on the bank.

The scarab lay on the canal bank amongst the mud. After a while, as the mud dried in the sun, it rolled a little way and settled right in the middle of the tow path. There were voices in the distance – people coming along the tow path. The scarab lay in wait. For thousands of years people had been trying to destroy it. But the scarab was stronger than any of them. It had survived many disasters. It had caused many disasters. Now it waited on the tow path – waited for its next victim.

paradise loft

alison leonard

To everyone else, it was The Attic. But to Jenny it was Paradise Loft.

The stairs were steep and narrow. Long ago, when she was tiny and learning to talk, Jenny had said to Gran, 'These steps are *tight*.' Tight they were, like arms that could hold you as you lifted one little leg on to the next wooden step and brought the other one up to join it.

Now she ran up them – fast, breathless, scared – one, two at a time. She heard *their* scampering steps running after her up the carpeted flight below. *Them!*

At the top, she grabbed hold of the door handle, flung open the door, fell through, slammed it shut, and turned the stout, cold key.

Paradise.

They could bang-bang-bang up the tight bare stairs behind her. They could rattle-rattle-rattle at the handle of the door. They could shout, 'Jenny! Pig! Toad! Coward!' and then whimper, 'Come *on* … We didn't *mean* it …'

And she, Jenny, could be quiet. Absolutely still.

That was the power of it. They didn't understand that: how she could be quiet, and still, and alone, and be in paradise.

The room was enormous, and mostly empty. At the far end was a dormer window that threw a box of brightness on to the floor, complete with dark ribbons tying its parcel of light across and down. Jenny didn't ever go and stand in the window, because if she did she might be seen from outside, and wouldn't be alone any more. If she stayed in the shadow, away from that box of light, she could be private.

In the corners stood little old book-cases with rows and

rows of little old books. The walls – well, you couldn't call them walls, because the straight bit only went up to Jenny's waist. After that they were slopes, stretching right up to the peak in the middle. Along the sides, under the slopes, lay ancient trunks and canvas bags and suitcases. Some lay on their backs, some were propped on their sides, some had been shoved unthinkingly upside-down. What was inside them? Old love-letters, tied criss-cross with ribbons? Dolls with cracked china faces and torn lace frocks?

Jenny touched the top of one trunk, and pulled her finger away smudged with dust. She wrote in the dust: 'Jenny B hates –' Then she stopped. This was Paradise. She couldn't write their horrible names here. She scrubbed out the words, then stared at her filthy finger, took out a hankie and cleaned it with lots of spit.

But it was the floor that she loved most of all. That floor was the floor of paradise.

It too was covered with dust. But under the dust lay a whole world. Someone had painted a world there. Someone who possessed endless time – who had no one to rattle and whimper at the door. Someone with no Gran to call out, 'Where *are* you, Jennifer? It's time for tea!' Someone who could bring up a full tin of biscuits and a tall bottle of lemonade and stay, quietly, on and on, all day. Someone who first drew outlines with black pen or paint, and then chose a colour – blue, grey, green, yellow – and painted, carefully, with an eye for detail and a passion for correctness, a paradise, flat on the floor of the loft.

Jenny listened. They'd stopped shouting and whimpering. They'd gone away – given her up. Maybe they would go to Gran and say, 'Gran, we're worried about Jenny. She's locked herself in the attic. Maybe you should go and get her down.' But Gran, as always, would be busy. She'd say, 'Oh, run off and play and don't make such a fuss.'

Jenny tiptoed across from the trunk to the middle of the room. She shuffled her feet to clear a space in the dust on the floor, sat down and crossed her legs. She breathed in deeply, and held her breath. Then, leaning down as close to the floor as she could, she blew.

The dust lifted, and the air carried it up high in great arcs. Where the motes of dust hit the box of light from the window, it looked like a vast flock of faraway birds in the sunset. Quickly, before it could settle, she blew again. Then she shuffled round to her left and blew again, and shuffled and blew and shuffled again and blew again till she was facing the way she'd begun.

She was sitting in a paradise ring.

Now she looked with new eyes. She could see that she was sitting in the middle of a lake. She must be in a boat.

No, she was on an island. It was a small green-and-grey rocky island, with crops of gorse and heather, and a few fawn-coloured sheep. The lake was blue, with little white wrinkles for waves. Round the edge of the lake were reeds, and inlets, and pebble beaches, and wide mouths where streams ran in from distant hills.

Along one side of the lake ran a little road. Sometimes it was hidden by a wood or copse, sometimes it ran alongside the lake. There was a beach where she'd love to go swimming, and some rocks where it would be good to sit and fish. On the side opposite the road lay a meadow of tall rustling grasses, with flowers growing amongst them: violets and daisies, asphodels and pimpernels, buttercups and columbine. Tiny birds fluttered above the meadow, darting through the tall fronds and then out over the water like fishing lines thrown out and then drawn back.

At the edge, among bulrushes, minnows in their thousands rippled through the water just beneath the shining surface.

What was behind her? Jenny turned her head.

Across the water was a tall dark cliff. Seagulls and gannets nested in its crevices, and clefts with waterfalls plunged down to the lake below.

And a great arched cave opened its mouth towards her. The water lapped in and out, getting darker and darker as it disappeared into the cavern.

She wanted to swim over to the pebbled beach and go fishing from the rocks. The meadow, too, would be blissful. She would love to lie among the soft grasses and reach down with a jamjar to catch ten or twenty of the thousand rippling minnows.

But the cave! That great dark mouth was mysterious. The lapping water murmured to her as it disappeared into the cavern: 'Come. Come here. Come to me. Come.'

She found a small brown boat tied to a post in a little rocky cove, with two oars restling against the sides. Jenny had never ever rowed a boat before, but she stepped into it and sat down on the middle seat. Easing the boat off the pebbles into the open water, she started to row.

It was a long haul from the island to the cliff. She had to keep on turning round to see the way. Her arms were tired by the time the boat slid into the cave mouth, and her legs were stiff from pushing against the bottom of the boat.

She felt as if she was slipping into the huge jaw of a whale that was only too ready, only too eager, to swallow her up in one gigantic gulp. But the waves, lapping against the sides of the small brown boat, whispered, 'Row on! Row a little more!'

'What's inside the cave?' Jenny asked them.

'Row!'

'But I'm scared!'

'Row on!' lapped the waves. 'Row on!'

Hesitantly, dipping the oars only just beneath the water, she steered the boat under the great arch of the cliff. As the boat slipped deeper into the cave, the sun slipped away from her as if it were slipping off the edge of the world. The world was a balloon of light that got smaller and smaller and smaller. She was slipping out of light, and into darkness.

Her heart thumped – boom, boom, boom – against her chest.

Voices called to her. They uttered sounds that seemed to come from deep down inside the earth. 'Go back!' they called. 'Turn back – or take the risk!'

But the waves rippled round her: 'Row on – row on!'

Now, all her eyes could see in the gloom was the dark weed that floated past her on the surface of the darkening water. Her feet were tired with pressing against the bottom of the boat – her legs were tired with pushing – her arms were tired with rowing. She felt paralysed with tiredness, and her mind felt frozen with fear.

But, though she hardly wanted them to, her arms went on rowing, steadily, and her legs went on pushing, and her feet went on pressing on the bottom of the boat. It was as though the boat itself was being pressed, deeper and deeper. Softly the boat moved on, sucked into the cavernous mouth.

The cavern walls were damp. They dripped wet drops onto her hair. Dripping stalactites hung from jutting arms of rock. A thicker, stickier weed now trailed along beside the boat. Could fish be lurking below, opening their poisonous jaws to swallow her up? Or did monsters lurk here, that with a single heave could upturn the tiny boat and – whoosh! – engulf her in their tentacles?

The water dripped and echoed: 'Plip-plip! Dip-trip! Slip-flip! Skip-tip!' Beneath her, the sound of lapping had stopped. She held her breath. Even the water seemed to hold its breath.

Exhausted, Jenny let the oars drift. She shivered. In front of her, the mouth of the cave was a distant, unreachable circle of light. Behind her was darkness.

She must turn the boat round. She must leave the circle of light, and turn and face the darkness.

With her left oar, she paddled carefully, so that the boat slid round and faced the other way, into the unknown.

What were those points of light in the heart of the darkness? Were they the eyes of a great cave creature, staring at her? Panicking, she turned to left and right. The eyes were here – and there – and there ... Everywhere. Never ending.

She had met the monster of a thousand eyes.

She was tiny and alone. The monster was huge, and everywhere. It could swallow her up in an instant and she would never be seen again.

'Who are you?' she called. Her voice was trembling.

'Who are you-ou-ou?' answered the monster.

'I'm Jenny! Where do you come from?'

'Where,' it answered, 'do *you* come from?'

Jenny didn't want to answer that. The cave was a place of horrors, where she mustn't mention the name of Paradise.

'What kind of place do you live in, deep in there?' she asked.

'Deep in a lair, a lair, a lair!' came the reply.

Jenny felt the hair prickling at the back of her neck. Her forehead was damp and cold, and letting the oars rest for a moment, she put her hand up to wipe it. Despite the chill and the damp of the cavern, she was sweating with fear.

A lair? That was where beasts of prey lived, and dragons, and creatures who fed on living flesh. But still she was paralysed. She knew there was one more question she had to ask.

'Why did you want me to come into the cave? Why did you want to see me?'

'See me! See me!'

At last she knew the real answer – the voice was an echo. Of course!

But knowing that was no comfort, no comfort at all. If the voice was the echo of her own voice, then the monster was an echo of another monster – the one that hid inside herself.

She felt wet on her cheeks now, and it wasn't sweat, but tears. 'I want to go back to Paradise!' she cried. There. She had said the word.

The monster echoed it. 'I want to go back to Paradise!'

'No!' cried Jenny. 'Paradise shouldn't have monsters in it!'

'Monsters in it!' pleaded the echo.

'No, no, please!'

'*Please!*'

She had to take it with her. She couldn't row the boat back to Paradise until she allowed the monster from the deep to come into the boat with her.

But how? The monster was already there, inside herself, as well as on the outside. If she spoke, it spoke. If she stayed silent, it was silent too. But still she knew she must invite it to come. Otherwise, some part of her would stay forever inside the cave, away from Paradise.

Monster or no, she would invite it. 'Come on,' she called. 'Come *on*.' She sounded impatient, like her Gran did when she was calling Jenny to get ready for tea.

'I don't want to come,' answered the voice, irritatedly.

But she knew the monster must get into the boat. She grabbed hold of it. The monster wriggled and struggled. It was enormous, it would sink the boat, she would drown! But she knew she must pull it in beside her. She pulled, it wriggled – she pulled, it struggled – water splashed and flew … then, suddenly, the monster was inside the boat. It settled in and fitted perfectly. Jenny put her feet on it where it lay quietly. She picked up the oars and began to row.

She rowed furiously, as if her life depended on it. Breathless, she still had enough breath to say, crossly, 'But why did you ask me into the cave in the first place? Why, why?'

Faint and disappearing came the echo. 'High – high – high!' Then, even fainter, 'High … high!'

High?

Jenny looked up and saw, high above her, a hundred thousand – no, a million stars. Her fast and furious rowing had, at that moment, swept her out of the mouth of the cave and into the open lake. It was night. A warm breeze floated across from the hills. The stars were reflected in a million sparkling waves. The moon had risen and spread a path of molten silver across the shimmering lake.

Just as, deep inside the cave, the brightness of the sunlit world had shrunk to a tiny unreachable circle of light, so the cold dark mouth of the cave now shrank to a ball of darkness, then to a pinhead, and then to nothing as she gazed.

She and the boat drifted back across the shining water. The stiffness in her legs vanished, and her arms lay relaxed against the oars. When she heard the crunch of the boat on the pebbles of the shore, she jumped out and tied it up just as it was before.

Jenny sat on her island. Around her lay the dark blue

lake, and beyond that, Paradise.

She gave a little puff, and the dust blew. 'I'm Jenny,' she said to the dust. 'And I live in Paradise Loft.'

The dust hung in the air.

She spoke to the monster, wherever it was. 'And who are you, may I ask? Are you a many-eyed monster, or an echo, or just a million specks of dust?'

Feet thundered up the wooden stairs outside. The door-handle rattled and fists sounded – bang bang bang! – on the door.

'Jenny!' came the shouts. 'Don't be such a toad! A pig!'

Jenny stood up and went over to the door. She turned the cold stout key in the lock, and opened it.

'I'm not a pig or a toad,' she said to them. 'And I'm not a coward, either. I'm famished. What's the time? It's got to be time for tea!'

clownface

john gatehouse

1

Danny Lewis was helping his father to clean out the attic of their new house. The last owners had left in a hurry, in the middle of the night, and had never been heard of again.

The attic had a horrible musty smell, and it was filled with all kinds of rubbish. In a corner, buried under a pile of rotting clothes, Danny found a large plastic doll that looked like a clown.

It was about half his size, with a white-painted face and red nose. The doll was dressed in brightly coloured baggy clothes and big black shoes.

'What an ugly thing,' said his dad. 'It looks as if it's sneering at us. You can have it if you want, Danny.'

'Not likely!' said Danny, embarrassed. 'I'm too old to play with dolls.'

Danny threw the doll in the dustbin.

The next day, he packed his sports bag, ready for the first day of the new school term. He put in his pencils, pens and notebook, and the vest and shorts he wore for PE.

Danny was dreading school. Last term he had had an argument with Glenn Harding, the class bully, and had come off worst in the fight. He knew Glenn still held a grudge, and was out to get him.

Glenn was waiting outside the school gates when Danny arrived.

'Didn't think you'd come back, Lewis,' he growled, blocking Danny's path. 'Not after the thumping I gave you last time.'

Danny stepped back.

'Leave it out, Glenn,' he said nervously, his words coming out in a stutter. 'I don't want any trouble with you.'

'Well, you've got it!' said Glenn, snatching the bag from his hand.

'Hey! Give it back!' shouted Danny.

Glenn emptied the bag onto the pavement. Out fell Danny's pens, pencils, notebook, his vest and shorts …

… and the plastic clown doll.

2

Danny stared at the doll in amazement. He was certain he had thrown it away, yesterday.

So how had it got inside his sports bag?

'Ahh, isn't that sweet?' scoffed Glenn, shaking the doll in front of Danny's face. 'Lewis has brought his dolly to school!'

Danny could feel everyone watching him. He could hear giggles coming from a group of girls. His face stung from embarrassment.

'Give it here!' he cried, trying to snatch the doll from Glenn.

Glenn pushed Danny away. He tripped over his bag and fell to the ground, banging his elbow. Now everyone began to laugh.

Miss Turner, Danny's teacher, came hurrying up.

'What on earth is going on?' she demanded, looking first at Danny and then at Glenn. 'I hope you two aren't fighting again?'

Glenn smiled. 'No, miss. I was just admiring Danny's dolly when he fell over his bag.' He threw the doll down beside Danny. 'I'll see you later, Lewis,' he hissed, before walking off.

'Well, don't lie there all day, Danny,' said his teacher, crossly. 'The school bell is about to ring. Pick up your belongings and hurry up into class.'

Danny waited until his teacher and the other children had gone. He collected up his school equipment and shoved them roughly into his bag.

He was furious. That stupid doll had already ruined his day. Glenn would be teasing him for weeks about this.

Kicking it into the gutter, he hurried into the school.

First lesson was PE, Danny's favourite. He loved the climbing ropes and the trampoline. And best of all, Glenn wasn't in the same class. He was out playing football.

When the lesson had finished, Danny quickly dressed back into his uniform and returned to his class.

The doll was sitting on his desk.

3

Glenn was sitting at the back of the class, smirking.

'You rotten ratbag!' screamed Danny. 'You just can't stop picking on me.'

He picked up the doll and threw it at Glenn with all his might.

Now it was Glenn's turn to explode. He leapt out of his chair and grabbed Danny by his shirt.

'Look, pipsqueak! I didn't put the doll there! It must have been someone playing a joke!' He pushed Danny back against his desk. 'But now you really are going to get a beating! I'll be waiting for you in the playground at break. And you'd better be there!'

Miss Turner walked into the room.

'All right, you two!' she snapped, walking over to them. 'What's the matter now?'

Glenn happily told her about Danny throwing the doll at him.

'Is this true, Danny?' Miss Turner demanded.

Danny looked down at the floor. 'Yes, miss,' he said in a whisper.

'I've had enough of this silly bickering,' Miss Turner said sharply. 'One more disruption from you, Danny, and I'll be keeping you in after school. Now SIT DOWN!'

Danny picked up the doll and returned to his desk. He was about to drop it on the floor, planning to throw it away at breaktime, when he glanced at its face. The doll's features had changed. It wasn't sneering any longer.

It was scowling.

When the bell for break sounded, Danny stayed back in the classroom. If he went outside, Glenn would be waiting for him. He could see him through the window, standing at the top of the steps that led to the playground.

Danny felt angry. It was all that stupid doll's fault.

He turned around to kick it across the classroom ... and found that the doll was no longer on the floor by his desk.

4

Danny frowned. The doll had been there, only moments ago. He was sure of it.

So where was it now?'

Someone might have come in and taken it, but Danny was sure he would have heard them. And the doll couldn't possibly have walked off by itself. Could it?

'I hope I never see the horrible thing again,' he thought as he walked out of the classroom.

The corridor was busy with children, queueing up at the tuck shop. Danny usually liked to buy a bar of chocolate to keep him going until lunchtime.

But not today. His stomach felt like it was tied in knots.

He knew that Glenn was outside, waiting to thump him. Danny didn't mind a fair fight, but Glenn was much bigger and stronger than he was.

'Come along, Danny,' said Miss Turner sharply. 'If you're not buying anything today, then go out to the playground. I can't have you cluttering up the corridor.'

It was useless to argue. Miss Turner had never liked him, and after this morning, she would be in no mood to listen to his side of the story.

With a sick feeling in his stomach, he pushed open the double doors and stepped outside.

Glenn was still standing at the top of the steps. He made a fist and smacked it into the palm of his hand.

Danny knew what that meant.

He looked the other way. Perhaps he could run off until break was over? No, Glenn would chase him until he was caught, and then he would get an even harder beating.

Suddenly, there was a loud cry. Danny looked up at where Glenn had been standing.

But he wasn't standing any longer.

He was falling through the air.

He struck first one concrete step and then another.

He lay at the bottom of the steps, holding his arm and crying.

Danny's doll was lying beside him …

… and it was smiling.

5

A group of children had gathered around Glenn. They were all looking at Danny, as if blaming him for the accident.

Miss Turner came running up.

'What's going on?' she demanded. 'What's happened to Glenn?'

Glenn pulled himself up, and gave a cry of pain. 'My arm!' he screamed. 'It's broken!'

Miss Turner ordered one of the children to fetch the matron.

'What happened?' she asked Glenn. 'Did you fall?'

'I was pushed!' cried Glenn, glaring up at Danny through tear-filled eyes. 'Danny pushed me!'

'He's lying!' shouted Danny. 'I was nowhere near him.'

Miss Turner's face grew red with anger.

'You're the one who's lying!' she snapped. 'I know how much you two hate each other. But you've gone too far this time, Lewis.'

'But I didn't push Glenn! Honest!' Danny protested.

Miss Turner ignored him. 'Go back to class, Danny!' she said. 'I'll be phoning your father. And you will be staying behind after school for detention. I'm not having bullies in my class!'

Danny walked back into the school. He felt light-headed, as if he were about to faint. It wasn't fair. He was being punished for something he didn't do.

Then he remembered the doll.

He ran back outside. Glenn was being helped by matron towards her office.

Miss Turner had gone.

And so had the doll.

Had Miss Turner picked it up? Or had it walked away by itself?

Danny felt a chill run down his back.

'Where's Miss Turner?' he asked a boy.

'She's gone to the store room to fetch some books,' replied the boy.

Danny ran back into the school, pushing people aside. He had just reached the store room when he heard a loud crash and a strangled cry from inside.

Pulling open the door, Danny peered into the room.

Miss Turner was laying crumpled up on the floor, unconscious. An overturned stepladder lay next to her. Books were scattered all over the place.

In a corner of the room sat Danny's doll ...

... and there was an evil smile on its clown face.

6

'Miss Turner has had an accident,' the headmaster told the pupils who had crowded into the hall for an urgent meeting. 'She must have slipped off the stepladder and fallen.'

There was much whispering and gasps of surprise from the children.

'She has recovered consciousness, but she will be kept in hospital for a few days,' the headmaster went on. 'I know many of you are upset about this accident, so I have decided to finish school early today. You may all go home.'

There were a few cheers at this news, and the children quickly bundled out of the hall.

Danny didn't feel like cheering.

He believed the doll was alive.

Glenn had bullied him, and had met with an accident. Miss Turner threatened him with detention, and had met a similar fate. And each time, the doll had been there.

Smiling, always smiling.

Danny had already picked up the doll from the store room and shoved it in his bag.

Running outside, he saw the skip that the school was renting. It was full of rubbish that had been left behind after the workmen had finished building the new classrooms. Pulling the doll out of the bag, Danny climbed up the metal steps to the top of the skip.

Glancing around to make sure no one was looking, he threw the doll into the skip. Then he reached in and pulled a number of heavy rubbish bags on top of it.

Once he was sure the doll could not escape, Danny walked back home.

He felt relieved. That was the last he would see of it.

7

Danny's father was setting light to a bonfire in the back garden when he arrived home. All the rubbish from the attic was piled up, waiting to be burnt.

Danny watched the flames catch light to an old armchair. Puffs of grey smoke drifted high into the air.

He told his father about Miss Turner's accident, but he didn't mention anything about the doll. He wanted to forget all about it.

'Well, since you've got the afternoon off, you can help me clear out the house,' said his father.

Danny worked until late in the evening, carrying out old furniture for his father to throw on the bonfire. The bonfire was still blazing away when it was time for him to go to bed.

Danny brushed his teeth and changed into his pyjamas.

He climbed into bed and tried to fall asleep. But each creak and groan of the old house set his nerves on end. He kept jerking awake, expecting to find the doll sitting in a corner of the room.

'I'm being stupid,' he muttered, laying his head back down on the pillow for the fifth time. 'That doll couldn't be alive. I must have been imagining it all. And even if it was, it can't get to me now.'

Danny finally drifted off to sleep.

An owl hooted somewhere in the night.

Outside, a dark shape moved quickly through the long grass.

It stopped beneath Danny's open window. Putting both hands around the drainpipe, it began to climb.

8

Danny woke up with a start. He could feel something heavy moving on top of his duvet.

His mouth went dry. He wanted to bury his head under the blankets, the way he used to when he heard strange noises in the night.

He slowly lifted up his head.

Standing at the bottom of the bed was the clown doll. It was covered in dirt and grime.

The doll wasn't smiling now. It was glaring at Danny.

And it held a rusty screwdriver in its hand.

Danny's heart began to pound. His palms felt sweaty.

He pushed back the covers and rolled off the bed, just in time.

The clown leaped forward, burying the screwdriver into Danny's pillow.

Danny tried to cry out for his father, but he was so scared, he couldn't speak.

The clown turned, sneering at him.

Grabbing the night lamp off the bedside table, Danny swung it with full force, smashing it into the doll. The doll flew across the room and crashed into the wall. It rolled over and stood up, still holding the screwdriver.

The doll was blocking Danny's escape through the door.

He turned. As quickly as he could, he clambered out of the window. Grabbing hold of the drainpipe, he began to climb. The wind whipped at his face.

Looking down, he could see the doll scrambling up the drainpipe after him.

Danny pulled himself onto the roof.

There was nowhere to hide.

He was trapped.

9

The doll climbed onto the roof. Its face was full of anger.

'Go away!' whispered Danny. 'Leave me alone!'

He stepped back, and slipped on the tiles.

'Help!' he cried, as he slid down the roof. In desperation, he grabbed hold of the metal guttering. It creaked and groaned under his weight.

The doll, smiling now, walked across to where Danny was hanging in midair.

It raised its big foot to stamp on Danny's fingers.

Letting go of the gutter with one hand, Danny grabbed hold of the doll's leg. Pulled off balance, the doll let go of the screwdriver. It sailed past Danny's face, grazing his cheek.

Praying he wouldn't fall, Danny threw his arm backwards and let go of the doll. Without a sound, the doll sailed through the air and landed on top of the burning bonfire.

Using both hands, Danny pulled himself back onto the roof. He sat shaking and crying at the same time. Looking down, he could see the doll's plastic clown face melting in the flames.

'Good riddance!' he shouted, a sudden rush of happiness making him giddy.

Then he heard the voice.

'Danneeee! Danneeee! I'll be baaaaaaccckkk ...'

It was the wind, Danny told himself.

Just the wind.

dolphin story collections

chosen by **wendy cooling**

1 top secret
stories to keep you guessing by rachel anderson, andrew matthews, jean richardson, leon rosselson, hazel townson and jean ure

2 on the run
stories of growing up by melvin burgess, josephine feeney, alan gibbons, kate petty, chris powling and sue vyner

3 aliens to earth
stories of strange visitors by eric brown, douglas hill, helen johnson, hazel townson and sue welford

4 go for goal
soccer stories by alan brown, alan durant, alan gibbons, michael hardcastle and alan macdonald

5 wild and free
animal stories by rachel anderson, geoffrey malone, elizabeth pewsey, diana pullein-thompson, mary rayner and gordon snell

6 weird and wonderful

stories of the unexpected by richard brassey, john gatehouse, adèle geras, alison leonard, helen mccann and hazel townson

7 timewatch

stories of past and future by stephen bowkett, paul bright, alan macdonald, jean richardson, francesca simon and valerie thame

8 stars in your eyes

stories of hopes and dreams by karen hayes, geraldine kaye, jill parkin, jean richardson and jean ure

9 spine chillers

ghost stories by angela bull, marjorie darke, mal lewis jones, roger stevens, hazel townson and john west

10 bad dreams

horror stories by angela bull, john gatehouse, ann halam, colin pearce, jean richardson and sebastian vince